I0710200

The Cat Who Hated Bird

Jay Chesters

The Cat Who Hated Bird

Radical Bookshop and Press
4838 Richard Road SW, Suite 300
Calgary, AB T3E 6L1

FIC029000 - Fiction, Short Stories

June 1, 2024

Editor: Nadine Brito
Cover Design: Lexie Angelo

Typeset in Kings Caslon

ISBN-13: 978-1-990201-17-2

Printed in the United States

For Cass. You're the cat's knees.

contents

CHAPBOOK

The Cat Who Hated Bird

It's the end of the world, and I can't find my car keys. That would be funny, if it weren't true.

It goes like this—a military escort arrives at my front door in fifteen minutes. I must be waiting.

When the military escort arrives, I must be waiting with my bags packed.

When the military escort arrives, I must be waiting, bags packed, and Miles in his cat carrier.

When the military escort arrives, I must be waiting, bags packed, Miles in his cat carrier, and the house secure. Car loaded. Ready to go.

I repeat the instructions to myself over and over. I suddenly remember being six years old, sitting in a circle on the scratchy carpet floor of my primary school classroom. It all feels like a hundred years ago, and I wonder what became of the other kids in my class.

I remember we were playing a memory game that involved a list of things bought from the supermarket. Every kid repeated what the previous kids bought and then added something new at the end.

The list got longer and longer as you went around the circle. I'd try to remember everything, but I was distracted. I kept trying to think of the best item to add on my turn.

I went to the supermarket, and I bought a banana. I went to the supermarket, and I bought a banana and a bicycle. I went to the supermarket, and I bought a banana, a bicycle, and a place in a doomsday bunker—I should focus. The military escort will wait for exactly five minutes. If I'm not ready, I'm on my own. Good luck reaching the bunker that way.

That's why I prepared early. Bags packed, car fuelled—all ready for nearly a week. Packing for the end of the world is slightly different than packing for a weekend away. You get exactly two bags, you can't pay for extra baggage, and you definitely won't be able to buy anything you've forgotten later.

There must be washing machines. Facilities of some kind. But I suppose they don't print brochures for apocalypse bunkers. No one is going to have details for this sort of scenario.

We've known about the *potentially hazardous object* for months and I don't remember when it stopped being *potentially* hazardous. It was officially designated (*800815*) *1980 DA* because they don't give these objects human names the way they do tropical storms. Not *Doomsday Meteor Wendy* or anything like that. But everyone calls it the world killer. There is nothing anyone can do.

All we have are bunkers. It turns out most countries have them: whole networks of tunnels and bunkers in case of war, viral pandemic, Christmas pageant gone awry, or any other kind of large-scale disaster. The bunkers are vast, but there is nowhere near enough space for everyone. This is how the world ends, and all that.

El, also variously called Elizabeth, Ellie, or Ella, qualified us both for the bunker because she's a senior plant biologist for the Department of Agriculture. "The Ag", as she calls it. The world needs people like her, but I come as part of the package; partners and pets.

The powers that be made it abundantly clear that if you're not with a military escort, you're not getting in any bunker. I *must* be ready. And find my bloody car keys.

We're only driving my car to the bunker because we sold hers last year. We wanted to do our bit towards saving the planet. Look where that's got us.

"Diz, are you still looking for your car keys?"

El is a sentry in the bedroom doorway as I rummage through my battered rucksack for the tenth time.

"No, I've already found them. I keep looking because I enjoy feeling judged by you."

"You're a grown-up, Daisy. Why don't you always put them in the same spot?" Things get serious when El drops my nickname Dizzy and starts calling me Daisy.

"I don't know, El, but making me feel bad about it is definitely helping things."

"We've fifteen minutes until the escort gets here. He won't wait."

"You're sure he won't come in for a coffee? Maybe the four of us can watch TV."

"Miles isn't a person, Daisy. He's a cat."

I'm suddenly aware of the dull ache that runs all the way up the side of my face. I've been unconsciously grinding my teeth. But I say nothing about the snub to Miles. One argument at a time is about all I can keep track of.

"El, can you help me look?"

"Have you checked the kitchen?"

"Why would they be in the kitchen?"

"I'm only asking if you've *looked*. Where's the spare?"

"Lost it, months ago."

"You *lost* it?"

"Yes. I lost it. Months ago. Maybe not lost-lost, but I can't find it. Didn't seem like a big deal."

"You realise that's needed if you want replacement keys?"

"The world is ending, El. I don't think that's important."

El becomes a dark thundercloud as she turns away, sweeping out of the room and down the stairs. Doors slam as she approaches the kitchen. I wince as the picture frames in the hallway rattle.

I know how this sounds, but I need you to understand that El is a lovely person.

She's kind. Funny. Incredibly smart. She loves painting, she's been learning to dance, and I fully understand that I absolutely drive her up the wall. El doesn't even have a short fuse, she's got a surprisingly long fuse. You need one living with me.

I'm convinced there are saints with less patience than El. The way I'm always losing things makes her mad. How I don't pay attention to things like a normal person. It wears me out too. That I can't be normal. As if I know what normal is.

The trouble is, I can't tell how close she is to exploding. Other than when I'm being sarcastic. Sarcasm is a surefire way to piss her off. I know that I'm hitting a big red "do not push" button when I use it.

Maybe that's not the only problem. It also bothers me that El dislikes cats. Calls them *manipulative*. I thought she was joking at first, but her eyes weren't laughing. She said they were vicious little killing machines. I corrected her and said they were cute, fuzzy little killing machines. She didn't find that amusing.

I think El became a plant biologist simply because she prefers plants to animals. She definitely likes plants more than she does humans.

But Miles is an inside cat, so he's not killing anything. Despite that, El hasn't warmed to him. They tolerate each other, and that's about it.

I think the real reason El dislikes Miles is that the cat hates jazz, particularly Charlie Parker. I'm told it may be something to do with how he played unusual notes outside the main key, but I don't understand anything about that kind of stuff.

Personally, I find it funny that Miles hates Charlie Parker. Charlie Parker, whose nickname was Bird. El doesn't see the funny side of a cat who hates Bird.

The mutual antagonism between Miles and El started on the night she moved in.

We'd spent the whole day moving, shuttling back and forth between El's house and mine with a moving van I'd hired. It might have gone quicker if I'd had any sort of plan or system for loading and organising the van.

By the evening, we were done and too tired to think, let alone cook. Sitting on the floor, we ate Chinese takeaway straight from the containers. I went to grab wine from the kitchen.

At that moment, Miles was curled up on the couch, asleep on a colourful patchwork blanket. He was doing this adorable thing I love: curling into a tight ball and covering his little nose with his tail so that I can't tell one end from the other. It's like he's a furry little black hole warping the space-time of the sofa.

El decided to change the playlist. If I'd known what El was doing, I would have thrown myself at her feet. Done anything to stop her.

I've thought about if things had gone differently. If she'd chosen something, anything, other than Charlie Parker. In a good mood, Miles tolerates Chet Baker's singing, but I've never risked playing Miles Davis.

The opening bars of the classic *Bird on 52nd St* drifted through the air.

There had been comings and goings all day, and Miles had been shut in the spare room for a few hours. I didn't want to risk him escaping and getting lost. I was proving to El that I was a responsible cat parent, not like the ones she hated.

Miles had been asleep for about ten minutes, and I was still searching for a corkscrew for the wine. Then I heard El scream.

From what I can piece together of the incident from El's accounts, she patted Miles, startling him awake. That's when he would have heard the jazz...honestly, it was nobody's fault.

El says Miles latched onto her wrist with all four paws and bit her. Hard. He let go as she screamed, fleeing to his safe place underneath my armchair.

From the kitchen, I couldn't tell what was happening. I didn't know El was hurt, so I called out "what are you doing to my kitten?"

You should have heard the language that came out of El's mouth. A pirate would be shocked by her creativity.

We cleaned El's bleeding, swabbed her with Dettol, and to be safe, took her to the hospital. She only needed a couple of sutures, a tetanus booster, and some antibiotics. Nothing too serious.

I've got a theory that El has been exposed to most things doing fieldwork, and a cat bite isn't anything to slow her down for long. It's not like being stung by the venomous gympie-gympie plant.

It's been four years since, but El and Miles haven't grown any closer. I think El resents that she can't play jazz without getting attacked by a raging cat, but everyone gets the same reaction. I've got a scar on my ankle from when I tried playing *Bird and Diz*.

It's uncanny. You have no idea where Miles is in the house, but you're certain wherever he is, he's surely asleep. You take a risk playing *One Night In Birdland* and then, out of nowhere, he appears.

A demon with amber eyes as wide as saucers, yowling like he's being tortured. It doesn't happen with any other type of music. Just jazz.

It's no surprise I lost my keys, I've got a lot on my mind. My work might not be important like El's, but my team of graphic designers is short two people, and we're on track for triple the job requests compared to last year.

We *were*. There's not so much demand for graphic design with the world ending, despite a brief boost in public service announcements. Have you ever considered the best font for expressing *Sorry, there's a meteor about to end all life on Earth?* I went with Cambria. It has the right kind of gravitas yet still feels accessible.

Design requests were still coming in right up until they sent everyone home. Someone might still want that outdoor advertising PVC banner.

I've often wondered why I always misplace things. Why I can't put things back in the same place. I put my phone down for a minute and then spend the next hour looking for it. Or I'm about to leave the house, and I *swear* I had my keys, so where are they?

I've got a theory. I think the house could be a kind of wormhole in time and space. I put things down, and they disappear, off to somewhere else in the universe. There's a remote planet out there where it rains molten lead, or diamonds the size of goose eggs. Maybe that's where my spare keys are?

Don't ask me how often I lose my car in car parks. I think someone follows me and moves it when I'm out of sight. There might be more occasions than I care to admit when I've been flat-out convinced my car was stolen.

I was *absolutely sure* it was on parking level yellow-five, and if not, it was definitely on blue-six. I finally found it on level purple-eight after methodically checking every single row on every single floor.

If I were me, and I put my keys somewhere, where would I have put them? Sometimes, this helps. I get that I *am* me, obviously, but I pretend it's as if I were someone else. My mind is that foreign country where they do things differently.

Maybe my keys are in the spare room!

I remember now: I brought Miles' cat carrier in from the garage, which had needed to be locked in case of apocalypse looters. I

14

even commented on the absurdity of locking up, because it's not like someone is going to want to steal a lawnmower or some solar-powered Christmas lights.

I put my keys on top of the cat carrier after I did this so that I wouldn't lose them. If I put the carrier down in the spare room, then maybe I didn't pick the keys up again.

El is probably still mad, but if I find my keys now, there's a chance everything is going to maybe be all right. Except for the world ending.

And you know what? Maybe it won't end. Some experts say there's a chance the meteor might be less dense than we think, or that the rocket they shot into it will have nudged it that tiny bit to be enough to miss us. Then, for most of the planet, the destruction it brings will be mostly survivable.

We'll be safe in the bunker either way. I don't want to think about the people who won't.

"Eight minutes!" El shouts from somewhere in the house. As if I needed that.

When I open the door to the spare room, a swift shadow races between my legs. Miles.

I forgot I'd shut him in with his carrier. It was only going to be until our bags were packed in the car. I could have put him in his carrier, but when he sings the song of his people, he sounds so mournful. You can't blame me for putting it off.

I didn't expect to have to look for my keys. But it's okay.

And *there they are*—on the floor, next to the cat carrier. Right where I dropped them. I even remember dropping them —I was going to drop something, and it was better to drop the keys rather than the carrier.

"I'll grab them in a minute," I told myself. It's funny that I remember now, but I completely spaced on picking them up in that moment.

Keys in hand, I wander downstairs, jingling them so El hears me coming. Her two bags are packed in the hallway, but the kitchen door is still shut.

I go in. El stands by the window, watching the birds as they hop about the birdbath in the garden. It's as if everything is normal.

"Found them, then?" It's more a statement than a question.

Sarcasm is incredibly tempting, but I've come to make peace.

"Yeah. Dropped them in the spare room earlier when I was
carrying Miles' crate." I won't mention that I *meant* to pick them up
but forgot.

She turns from the window, and I hand her the keys. Maybe it's
the physicality of finally having them in her hand that makes El's
shoulders relax. I know the fight was my fault—I don't want us to be
mad at each other when the world ends.

"I'm sorry I was cranky before."

"I'm sorry, too, Diz. I don't get why you're always losing things
or forgetting things. Like how you forgot you'd started running the
bath and flooded the landing."

"Can we not talk about that again? We've got about five minutes
until the end of the world, and I need to find Miles."

"What do you mean, *find* Miles? Isn't he in the spare room?"

"He was. Not now. Not since I opened the door. And because his
carrier is out, he thinks he's going to the vet, so he's performed his
famous disappearing act."

"Fuck's sake, Daisy, we don't have time for this shit."

I'm about to say Miles isn't *shit*, he's a cat, but I know El means
my bullshit. I've got a feeling I know where Miles is, anyway.

His first stop is usually the living room—whether he's hiding or
not. Leaving El, I take a quick look. There's no cat on the furniture.
I get down on my hands and knees and crane my neck, looking
under my armchair. Seeing a tumbleweed of dust and hair, it
occurs to me that maybe we should have cleaned. I don't suppose it
matters, given that the planet is going to be obliterated by a meteor.

"Miles, are you under here?"

Finding a black cat in the dark is difficult at the best of times.
Finding one that doesn't want to be found is infinitely harder.

I think maybe one patch of darkness looks slightly more inky
black than the rest. Is it moving? The longer I look, the harder it gets
to tell if it's my imagination.

My eyes adjust, and it's increasingly clear there's no Miles.
There's a chewed catnip mouse under the chair, a single ankle sock
with a hole in the heel, my favourite black sports bra, and the water
bottle that I thought I left at softball a month ago. But no cat.

In the street outside, things are getting hectic. Some people might
have left it a little late to decide they're going somewhere else. I'm
not judging anyone else for their poor advance planning.

16

I hear a large, noisy engine among the rest of the noise. For some reason, I thought our escort to the bunker would come in a sleek black car, but this sounds more like a battleship.

"Daisy!" El doesn't need to say anything else.

"I know!" I reply. She knows I do. I hear her open the front door, and while I can't hear what's being said, I can imagine the broad strokes.

Looking around the room, I scan for a hiding cat. Nobody sits on the windowsill behind the navy-blue curtains (but I notice somebody has been scratching them), nobody tries to blend in as a shadow on the multicoloured crochet blanket in the corner of the couch, and nobody pretends to be a raven on top of the jarrah bookcase.

The door to the hall closet is closed, so he isn't in there. That's a small blessing, at least; once Miles got shut in there and threw up in my favourite black Converse shoes. They haven't smelled the same since, and it makes formal occasions like gallery openings awkward.

I take one last look around the room. It's just furniture, yet I feel like I'll miss it. But I don't have time for sentimentality, I've a frightened cat to find.

The hallway is empty, and the front door is wide open. For a minute, I think El left without me, but as she walks through the door, I remember the obvious. If it weren't for her, everything would be a panic. I almost don't notice that El is accompanied by a woman in a spotless military uniform. She has a sensible haircut.

"Diz, this is Captain Nica," El says, like they're old friends.

"Hi, Daze," Nica says quietly. El raises an eyebrow at me.

Right about now, she's remembering I have an ex named Nica. I don't know if I mentioned to El that Nica was my first serious girlfriend after I came out. Or how Nica broke my heart. I know I didn't mention she was in the army.

In my defence, I don't know that I remembered, even if her basic training played a big part in us breaking up.

I'm certain that I didn't know she got made a Captain. Then again, we haven't talked in a decade, and honestly? I tried my hardest to forget her.

But now it's the end of the world, and my current partner, the woman I wanted to marry before this whole *extinction-level event*, is introducing my ex-girlfriend to me.

I didn't expect the end of the world to be like this, but nothing today is like what I expected.

"Ready to go?" Nica asks.

El sighs. "She's looking for the cat."

"Miles isn't just a cat—"

"—no, pets are family," Nica cuts me off. "You can say goodbye, but we're on a tight schedule."

"I know." El's voice is soft, though I'm unsure what she's agreeing to.

"Do you have a picture?"

I thought our escort wouldn't wait. Now Nica wants to look at cat pictures?

"Sure, yeah, one sec." I pull my phone out of my back pocket. It would have been helpful if I'd thought of using the phone torch when I was looking for Miles under the chair. "This is Miles. I took the photo last week because I like how his black fur looks sort of chocolate-brown in places in the sun. And this one," I scroll through an almost embarrassing number of photos of him. "Miles is asleep, but he's forgotten to put his tongue away."

"Cute," she says, but I can't tell if Nica is sincere. Everything she says has a clipped, business-like military tone.

"Daisy." I hear the full stop in Elizabeth's voice.

There's never any question how El feels. More often, it's the *why* that I'm likely missing. Like how I'm unclear why Nica speaks to me like we're practically strangers, or why she wants to look at pictures of Miles.

I don't even know what I'm supposed to call her. Captain? Captain Nica? Just plain Nica? She's the only 'Pannonica' I've ever known, though nobody other than her Mum ever used her full name. Never meeting anyone else named Nica has been helpful, up until now. Now, the shape of her name feels like stones in my mouth.

Are you allowed to call someone by their first name in a professional situation like this? Then the penny drops for me. *Captain* Nica wants to help find Miles, but she needs to know what she's looking for.

"An American shorthair black cat, with yellow eyes?" Nica acts like it's a question, but she doesn't bother waiting for a response.

"Have you looked under the furniture? That's commonly the first place cats go."

"Sorry, I mean, yeah," I trip over my words. "I mean, I looked in the linen room, and he's not there."

"Do you need someone to have a proper look?" El asks, and yeah, it's a reasonable question.

Often, I *do* need someone to take another look because I've been distracted and forgotten what I was looking for.

"No, I properly looked, he's definitely not there."

"Diz, we need to go." El has her watch turned to the underside of her wrist so she can't see it. She scuffs her feet on the floorboards and looks at Nica. "We need to go, right?"

Nica checks her watch before looking from El to me. She checks her watch again as though she wants to be certain of something. "I can give you two minutes. I get it. You need to say goodbye to your friend,"

"Thanks." I give Nica a small smile. At least she gets it.

Then her words sink in, and I realise what I didn't notice before.

"What do you mean, 'Say goodbye'? Miles is coming. I've got his carrier, and his food, and everything. I can find him. He's got to be somewhere."

"Ma'am, I think you're mistaken. There are no pets where we're going."

I hear her words, but they don't make any sense. It's like we're talking about two different subjects. The woman who broke my heart is standing in my hallway calling me ma'am, and I feel like there's some subtext I'm not picking up on. On some days, the whole world feels that way.

Instead, I automatically reply, my brain controlling my mouth without giving any conscious thought to the words.

"No, no, you're right, I mean, *yes*, you're right. There's been a misunderstanding. As you say, cats are family, Miles is my best friend, and El works for the Ag Department, and that's why we have this space for the three of us."

I'm talking too fast, but everyone keeps saying we're going to be late, and the words go on without me.

"We've had it all arranged for weeks, and—"

"—Miles isn't coming, Diz."

Right then, El's eyes are the most beautiful aquamarine, like a tidepool. Maybe she likes Miles after all.

"El, please, can you do the explaining, while I find Miles?"

"She's right, Diz, I'm sorry. I didn't know how to tell you. Honestly, I kinda hoped I could blame it on someone else. But Miles can't come."

"Look, I'm not being funny, but Miles is coming. We'll sort it out when we get there, or I'll secretly smuggle him in under my jacket."

"Daisy. Miles isn't coming, and if you try and force the issue, I'm fairly sure Captain Nica here is going to shoot you."

"I don't want to shoot anyone, Ma'am."

All this talk of shooting me is not reassuring. At all. Then El sighs.

"Diz, you've got less than thirty seconds. Find Miles, say goodbye, then get your arse the fuck back out here."

I feel like a child who's been told they can't bring their favourite plush toy to the beach. Except I'm not a child. I'm a forty-something-year-old woman, and I don't care what they say.

I'm finding Miles and stuffing that ratbag cat under my jacket until we get to where we're going.

Right then, I know where Miles is.

Of course I do.

I should have looked there in the first place, but with everything else, I wasn't thinking straight. I run to the bedroom, and drop to the ground, half-wriggling under the bed to look properly. There's shouting in the street outside, and doors slamming. But none of that is my problem. My sole concern is Miles.

Two guarded, golden moons gaze at me in the darkness under the bed.

Miles blinks slowly, and I blink back. I see why he likes it here; everything is peaceful. It's like the rest of the world doesn't exist. And in a little while, it won't.

"Hey, Miles, we need to go." I reach out. Miles sniffs my hand in case I come bearing treats, but I can't reach him.

"Come on, buddy." I hope he'll come out because I'm asking nicely. He doesn't move.

I breathe in and try to squeeze a little further forward under the bed. Miles watches warily. There's still a commotion outside, but it feels even further away.

"Mate, come on, let's go." Miles slinks further back as I try for the scruff of his neck.

If I can get a hand around his back, I might be able to encourage him to move. As I stretch, there's a sound like a thunderclap outside and a sudden, brief scream.

Miles flattens his ears. He'll take a chunk out of me if I touch him. "What now, buddy?"

I'm half-stuck under the bed, Miles won't come out, and even if he does, I think Captain Nica might have just shot someone in the street.

She said she didn't want to shoot anyone. Nica always was very careful with her words: she said she didn't *want* to, not that she *wouldn't*.

Things are quiet outside, and I worry, but Miles doesn't care. I hate that it's come to this, but I've no choice.

Getting out from under the bed is almost as hard as cramming myself half under it. I'm covered in dust, and who knows what the other survivors will think of me in this state.

On my way out of the room, I briefly consider shutting the bedroom door, but Miles isn't going to run into the street now. He's spooked and staying where he is.

We're way past due to leave, but they won't have left without saying something. El is mad at me, but she's still here. My feet are concrete blocks as I walk down the stairs, and I find myself stopping part-way and looking at the stair carpet, reflecting again how maybe we should have cleaned it. I remember last Christmas, and how I considered buying a garment steamer so I could try cleaning the stair carpet but didn't want El thinking it was meant as a gift for her.

It's funny the things that seemed important at the time. I will myself to keep moving, one foot in front of the other. I can't change anything now, so it's up to me to make the best of the situation and face ahead.

At the bottom of the stairs, the front door is open, and I freeze as I step into the street. It looks like a warzone. There's broken safety glass everywhere. A car is abandoned like a marooned tank in the garden bed of the house across the street, and I'm fairly certain that's someone's fresh blood on the pavement.

El is slumped against the truck. I have knives in my blood for a second, but then she looks at me, and I feel the tremendous weight of everything. She isn't bleeding, nor has she been shot. But her face is pale, and there are dark half-circles the colour of twilight under her eyes.

El commented to me one day that she felt like she was trapped in her life. It would have been eighteen months ago. Long before all of this.

I thought she meant trapped in her job, trapped in our house because we couldn't afford to move with interest rates and inflation as they were. These were the things we worried about before the world killer.

But maybe she felt trapped with me too? I need to make things right.

"No Miles?" El tries to smile. I genuinely love how she can joke when things are tough. Even about this.

I squeeze her hand. "Nah," I say. "Miles will guard the house for us. Keep the mice out."

I look up at the bedroom window, expecting to see Miles staring down, but it's empty. The house looks so small now.

"Besides, he said he didn't fancy having to stay inside my jacket."

"Nica would have shot you. She shot someone trying to steal the truck."

"No shit? I wondered what the noise was. Where's our friendly neighbourhood Captain now?" I might not have given El the full, unabridged version of the Nica breakup story, but I don't imagine that I'm fooling anyone by acting casual.

"She's over there. People are losing it." El nods in the direction of two more army trucks parked further down the street. A roadblock.

"I guess she has to explain what happened?"

"I'm not totally sure Nica can shoot civilians, though it's not like she *killed* him. It was more of a graze. It's scary, someone being that good a shot, able to get so close without accidentally hitting them."

I'm about to say something about how Nica can often get so close and then bite my tongue.

As if on cue, Captain Nica walks back towards us. She's too far away for me to see if she's angry, but I feel like she must be. How far behind schedule are we?

"Best get in the car, then. Our bags are already loaded."

"There's something I need to do, El. I'll catch up."

"Seriously, what the fuck, Daisy? No. Whatever you could possibly have to do—no. We're not waiting."

"I didn't say *wait*, I said I'd catch up."

"There's no bloody way you're catching up. Do you actually think they'll let you in the bunker alone? Don't be a child."

"No, El, please, really listen. You said recently you felt trapped, and I didn't realise it then, but you meant trapped with me. And I don't want you feeling trapped like that."

"I didn't say trapped with *you*, don't put words in my mouth. This isn't the bloody time, Daisy."

That El is now swearing with every other sentence and calling me *Daisy* speaks volumes. I'm lucky that Captain Nica didn't give El a gun while she waited with the truck.

"It's the only time there is. We can't pretend things are normal and go live in a bunker together while the world ends. You can't get more trapped than living underground with someone who makes you unhappy."

"I'm not having this conversation." El opens the driver's side door of the car and climbs inside.

"Need a hand with something?" Nica asks as she reaches us.

"I'm fine, thanks," El replies. "Tell Daisy to stop being a fuckwit and get in."

"You need to get in, Daze. We're leaving."

"I'm not coming. I told El, I'll catch up."

"It's all right, I already told her she's delusional."

Nica pauses, then says simply "Okay. Good luck."

"You're *not* bloody serious?"

Is El talking to me or Nica? I don't suppose it matters.

"See you later, El," I reply. Nica's already in the cab of her truck, starting the engine.

El stares straight ahead. Perhaps she's thinking if she looks at me, then she might not leave. I don't want to see El's oceanic eyes right now, or I might change my mind too.

The truck starts moving, then El starts moving, and I start moving too, dragging myself back to the house. I can tell the soldiers further up the road are watching. I can't let them think I'm interfering with anything. I go inside and shut the front door against the warm evening air.

As I head up the stairs, I have a brief moment of worry—what if Miles did come out from under the bed? Wandered into the street while I was talking to El? What if he's not here? As if it might make a difference, I start taking the stairs two at a time.

I'm almost running as I enter the bedroom and drop to the floor. My ribs were already sore from forcing half my body under the bed earlier, now I think I've bruised them worse, but I'll deal with it later. Or not.

Two watchful yellow globes blink at me in the gloom. Miles is still determined to stay where he is.

"Have it your way," I tell him, and I don't even try reaching out. I stand and brush the lint off my t-shirt.

Then I think, what does more dirty washing matter now? I take off the dusty t-shirt, throw it in the corner of the room, and pull on a clean one from the wardrobe.

As I go downstairs, I turn on every light. I used to do the opposite; I'd turn them off behind me as I went to save money. But I don't need to worry about the power bill now.

In the kitchen, I'd apparently forgotten I still had half a bottle of wine in the fridge. It should be about the right amount.

I pour a glass and then connect my phone to the living room's Bluetooth speakers. Make sure the volume is all the way up. Before I even reach my armchair, I've selected our entertainment: *Bird on 52nd St.* That should do the trick.

We've finished *52nd Street Theme* before I hear anything from upstairs. By the time the second track, *Shaw 'Nuff*, finishes, I hear a muffled miaowed complaint from somewhere in the house. Then the solid thump of a cat starting down the stairs. I'm starting to feel the wine.

We're barely into *Out of Nowhere*'s opening notes when Miles launches himself at me.

He goes straight for my legs. Trying to get the monster off me while simultaneously trying to stop the music earns me a scratch on the hand, but it's a light rebuke. A lucky one, as nobody is going to any hospitals tonight.

I change the music to some classic Pixies. Before I'm finished cleaning my hand with rubbing alcohol and putting a plaster on it, Miles is sitting in the middle of the living room rug, vigorously washing a back foot.

The biography of Caroline Herschel I was reading is still next to the armchair—wasn't I planning on taking that book with me? I'd have been disappointed if I got to the bunker and realised I'd forgotten it. At least now I might get to finish it. This chair has always been my favourite spot for reading. It's perfect as the late afternoon sun beams through the side window.

I'm still finding my place on the page when Miles jumps onto my lap. He turns in a circle three times, then settles down, purring like a diesel engine. I scratch under his chin, and rest my hand on his back as I continue reading where I left off. Miles is asleep almost instantly. Outside it's quiet now.

I don't know how long we have left. These things aren't an exact science and the end of *all* life on Earth is far from certain. Will we even know when it happens? Somewhere a car door slams. Miles lifts his head.

"It's ok," I tell him, "I've got you. There's nothing to worry about."

When the end finally comes, we're still there—and there's nowhere else in the world we'd rather be.

ACKNOWLEDGEMENTS

This book was written on Whadjuk Noongar boodja, and I acknowledge that sovereignty was never ceded.

Thank you to Cass for your belief and unwavering support.

Thanks also to Miriam Sullivan, Jonny Barrett, and Sam Gibson-Mayne for reading early versions of this story and being unafraid to give me honest feedback.

Thank you to Laura Keenan, Linda Martin, and Casey Mulder of Night Parrot Press for everything you do and give to the writing community, as well as for your encouragement and support.

Huge thanks to Lexie and Radical Books for everything you've done, not limited to taking a chance on this story. Also thanks go to Nadine Brito for championing this story and helping me sculpt it into its final form.

And finally, thank you to Charlie for being the best black cat in the world.

Jay writes unusual contemporary fiction, weaving together folklore and science fiction with fantasy, horror, and social commentary. Mostly intentionally. After 20 years of living in a dozen different cities across three continents, Jay now lives on Whadjuk Noongar Boodja (Perth, Western Australia) with his wife and two boisterous cats.

When he's not working, Jay is usually found in the wild in Perth's bookshops, cafes, and coffee shops, writing and making the place look untidy. When he's not writing, Jay generally frets about how he should be writing.

Jay really should be working on the difficult follow-up to his debut book, Year of the Bear. Fortunately, he has other works appearing in collections from Night Parrot Press and online in various places.

* 9 7 8 1 9 9 0 2 0 1 1 7 2 *